D1527385

A Circle in Time

A Regency Time Travel Romance

Book 3

Lisa Shea

Visit my website at LisaShea.com

~ v5 ~

Kindle ASIN B00NK3IBWI

print ISBN: 978-1502374592

Persevere.

A Circle In Time

Chapter 1

England, 1802

"All of this has happened before,
And it will all happen again."
-- James Matthew Barrie

Sorcha spit out a mouthful of slimy mud, struggling to push herself up. She was embedded in the foul-smelling goo at least several inches thick. It sucked tenaciously at her body as she rolled to break free of its grip.

Her head rang with echoes, and she had no sense of how long she had been sprawled there. Was it seconds? Minutes? Hours? A groan shook out of her as pain throbbed along the left side of her chest.

Jonathan's voice sounded from above, strong, urgent. "Sorcha! Stay put. I'm coming down for you." There was the sound of him climbing onto the wall. "Get over to one side if you can – these walls are slick. I might lose my grip. I don't want to fall on you."

Sorcha wanted to yell back that she was fine, but the most she could get out was a coughing rattle. It took her a moment to shake her head clear of the cobwebs. She gave up on speaking and carefully wriggled back against the side of the well. A sharp rock wedged against her rear, and she slid to the right, trying to find an angle where she wasn't in pain.

Dawn delicately added a sheen of golden highlights to the darkness. In its faint haze she could see that the bottom of the well was tumbled with jagged rocks, thick silt, oozing mud, a few copper coins, and other random detritus.

There was a noise from above. She swung her eyes up through the gloom. Jonathan was carefully, attentively, moving his way down the face, testing a handhold there, sampling several footholds before deciding on one to trust.

Sorcha tried again to call up to him. Her voice came out as a rough rasp. "Johnny, really, I think I'm all right. How about lowering down the bucket's rope? I'm sure I could climb up it to you."

Jonathan shook his head, reaching down with one hand for a fresh grip. "It's too weak. It'd snap like thread. Please, just –"

A screech sounded from above them, and Biddy was leaning over the edge. "My God! She's fallen in!"

Jonathan's voice held calm firmness. "Biddy, go get us a sturdy rope. Be sure to knot it every two feet."

"Hold tight – I'll be right back!" Her thundering feet faded into the distance.

He stretched down, tested a foot, then grunted as it slipped loose. He balanced for a moment on the other three grips, then reseated himself carefully on the new spot.

Sorcha's throat was tight. "Jonathan, please. Go on back up. I'll be fine until they come with the rope. There's no need for you to risk yourself."

"You could be hurt and just don't know it," he pointed out. "And it could take them a while to get the rope ready. Don't worry about me. I'll be fine, if I can just –"

He settled his foot onto an outcropping, testing it carefully, then looked up to check his grip on the rock above.

The sun shimmered, then crossed up over the edge of the well, sending blinding light into his eyes.

The rock beneath his foot gave way.

His arms spread-eagled back as he plummeted.

Sorcha's voice ripped out her soul. "Jonathan!"

Time seemed to suspend as he fell … spun … fell …

The entire well shook around her as he slammed, face-first, into the rock-laced mud.

Chapter 2

Sorcha stared at Jonathan's unmoving body in disbelieving shock. Then she scrambled over to his side.

"Jonathan! Jonathan!"

She knew moving him might be a risk, but with his face embedded deep into the mud she was more worried about him suffocating. As carefully as she could, she pushed up on his near shoulder to get him free. Then she rolled him over onto his back.

A solid layer of mud covered the entire front of his body, sealing his face as if he were a clay statue.

"Jonathan!" she cried again, then reached for the bottom of her dress and ripped loose a swath of fabric. She worked desperately on the area where his mouth should be and finally found those rich lips she cared for so much. She gently pressed them apart with her finger, then put her cheek down against the opening.

Nothing.

Tears were forming, flowing down her face, but she wouldn't give up. She worked next on the nostrils. She carefully brushed with her fabric rag, easing out the plugs of mud which had jammed into each opening. At last she had them clear. She lowered her cheek in front of them, hoping against hope for a faint sign of life.

Nothing.

The tears became a river.

She found his mud-caked hand and twined her fingers into it. She stared at that motionless mouth and began pleading.

"Jonathan, come back to me. I need you to come back to me. Wherever you are, whatever it takes, you follow my voice. Because I need you. I need you in this world with me. I can't do this alone."

Her throat closed up, and she began trembling. "Stay with me, Jonathan, I've only just found you, and you can't go now. You can't! Please … please … please …"

Sobs shook her, and she dropped her head in agony.

Pressure rippled through his fingers.

Her eyes popped open in desperate hope. "Jonathan!"

A cough, a sputter of mud, and he rolled on his side, hacking out the mud from his lungs. The coughing fit seemed to last an eternity.

At last he groaned and pulled up to sitting. His eyes met hers.

Without a word he drew her in. And then they were embracing, holding each other fiercely as if nothing could separate them again.

Sorcha was beyond thought. "Jonathan … Johnathan …"

He patted her on the back, rocking her gently from side to side. "I'm here," he reassured her, his voice rough. "I won't ever leave you again."

At last he sat back, blinking larger the two mud-holes in the mask that coated him. She could see the deep emotion that welled there. His voice was rough. "Sorcha, I am so, so sorry. You are stuck here now. You aren't where you wanted to be."

Brightness bubbled within Sorcha. "Don't worry about that. Not when you're all right. Nothing else matters right now."

Biddy's voice called from above them. "I've got the rope! We're sending it down!"

In seconds the end of the rope was curling in the mud before them. Jonathan pressed himself up to standing, then drew Sorcha up at his side. He looked up the rope. "It's not too far, but I'll tie it at your waist, just to make sure."

She shook her head. "I'm all right, really. It'll be faster if I just climb it." Her eyes twinkled. "You know I can do it."

He gave a wry smile. "Yes, I know you can do that, and anything else you set your mind to."

She flushed, then looked him over. "Are you sure you'll be able to come up after me?"

His grin grew. "Don't you worry about me. Up you go."

She wiped her muddy hands down on the few clean spots of her dress that she could find, and then tested the rope. It was sturdy and solid. She started her way up it, her feet braced on the well's side, going one step at a time. The well was indeed slick, but she took it carefully, and in a short while she was at the edge. Numerous hands pulled her over, and Biddy wrapped her up in a large, woolen cloak.

Her mother's voice came, shrill and harsh. "Jesus, Mary, and Joseph! After all the nonsense I've had to put up with you these past few hours, now you go falling into a well? I swear, Sorcha, when I get you back home –"

Lady Davenport gently but firmly interrupted her. "My dear Madeline, your daughter is alive and well. You should take comfort in that. Anything other discussion can wait for calmer times."

Madeline harrumphed, but apparently she was not willing to risk gain-saying her hostess.

Sorcha barely heard the conversation. She was turning to lean over the well's edge, to watch Jonathan's ascent. He looked like some sort of a mud golem come to life, but his hands were steady as he made his way up the rope's length. Each beat of her heart brought him one step closer to her.

Then, at last, he was standing before her. It took all of her strength not to fold herself into his arms again, not to lose herself in his strength. She wrapped her cloak tighter around her as Biddy stepped forward with wet towels.

He took one of the towels and dove his face into it, wiping away the mud and grime. He drew the towel away –

Sorcha gasped in shock.

The massive scar was not there.

Chapter 3

Lady Davenport echoed her gasp, but Jonathan's mother was looking at a thin stripe of red that traced from the top center of his forehead in an arc down to his right temple. "My God, Jonathan, you're hurt!"

Jonathan took a fresh towel and pressed it to his forehead, bringing it down to see the red impression. He gave a low chuckle. "Not to worry, mother. That's not a bad cut; it'll heal quickly enough."

Biddy's voice was warm. "Right he is. It'll leave a scar, that's for sure, but he'll be fine in a few days."

A scar.

Sorcha shook her head in confusion. It was as if her multiple worlds were overlapping and rearranging.

A Circle in Time

Jonathan turned his gaze to her, rich with a tangle of emotions - of concern, longing, and hesitation. "Sorcha, I -"

A sharp grip latched onto her wrist, and she cried out. Now her bruises had welts and her body was at its overload point. Her mother's voice pierced through the agonizing haze. "That is *it*, young lady. You nearly killed Master Davenport on his birthday. When I get you back home I swear I will –"

Jonathan's voice was steely, low, holding a menace that Sorcha had never heard before. "You will let Sorcha go. Right now."

Her mother's fingers flew off of Sorcha as if Sorcha was red hot. Madeline's mouth hung open in utter shock. And then she saw something in Jonathan's eyes.

She stepped back. Her mouth worked, but no sound came out.

Jonathan took a step forward, and Madeline stepped back again, her body rigid.

Jonathan moved to stand between Madeline and Sorcha. His voice was steely and crisp. "You will not lay one more finger on Sorcha, ever. She will be staying with us for the foreseeable future, until she decides what she wishes to do next with her life."

Madeline wrestled her fear into a sharp fury. "You can't do that! She's my child!"

"She's an adult," corrected Jonathan, "and she is free to do whatever she wishes."

Madeline craned to see Sorcha past Jonathan's bulk. "Sorcha, you come over here right this instant! I order you!"

Every sane portion of Sorcha's body craved to instantly comply. She knew what would follow if she disobeyed in the slightest. An entire childhood of beatings, of punishments, of daily abuse compelled her to obey or die.

And then Jonathan turned his gaze.

Those amber eyes were full of strength, of commitment, and certainty. She soaked them in, breathed them in as if they were the very air she survived on, and she spoke.

"I will be staying."

Madeline sputtered in outrage. "You will what? What did you say to me?"

Jonathan turned, the shifting of weight of a herd bull preparing to drive away an interloper with whatever force was necessary. "And I think it's time that you left."

Madeline opened her mouth, and again something she saw in his eyes brought her to a halt. She let out a growl, then turned and stomped across the garden.

Jonathan followed after her, and Sorcha went at his side, complete disbelief shining through every pore of her body. She hadn't actually said that, had she? She couldn't have done that incredibly risky, foolish act! Had she really just disobeyed a *direct order* from her mother?

The world was going to crash to a halt. Her mother would turn, grab her wrist, and her limbs would be shattered for sure. Her head would be shaved. Her fingernails removed. Her –

Jonathan nodded to the doorman as they approached. The servant swung the main door open, stepping aside as Madeline huffed through it. Fingers of dusk drifted through the crisp dawn air, wafting golden light on the line of carriages still waiting patiently along the street below.

Huddled on the bottom step was the vagrant they had seen when first coming to the party. It now seemed like years ago.

Madeline angrily kicked at him as she went past.

Jonathan turned to the doorman. "See that she gets safely home."

"Certainly, sir." In a moment the doorman was striding down the steps, following after Madeline with attentive purpose.

Sorcha blinked.

She was gone. She was really gone.

Sorcha could barely breathe it in. Had her entire life just changed? Was this a dream? Merely another vision that would vanish like fog on a winter's morn?

But here she was, with Jonathan at her side. And there her mother was, vanishing into the growing morning of Bath's new day. Sorcha had never been apart from her mother for a full day. Not once, ever.

The feeling of release thrilled through her, filled her, and she let out a joyful laugh.

The vagrant huddled tighter, pulling his hands over his head. "I'm so sorry, miss, I didn't mean to disturb your –"

Sorcha looked, blinked, and stepped out into the shimmering morning light.

"Hew?"

Chapter 4

Sorcha hurried down the steps to kneel at Hew's side. She could hardly recognize him. Before he had been burly, attentive, with a keen eye and a quick smile. Now he was rail-thin, hunched, shivering, and he cowered away from her in fear.

His voice was a tenuous plea. "I'm so sorry, miss. I didn't mean to do no harm. I'll move along, I promise."

There was a movement beside her, and Jonathan was there, staring at the man with a mixture of recognition and disbelief. At last he shook himself and turned his head. "Biddy, get the back room ready."

He stooped down and tucked one arm beneath Hew's back, the other under Hew's knees. Then he lifted Hew up in his arms as easily as if Hew was a small child.

Hew's shivering became more pronounced. "Please, don't hurt me, sir! I'll leave. I didn't mean –"

Jonathan's voice was warm and rough with emotion. "It's all right, Hew," he reassured the man, taking the stairs with careful attention. "We'll get you some food and drink. Calm yourself."

Hew groaned, as if he didn't believe it, but he relaxed back against Jonathan. He allowed Jonathan to carry him through the black-and-white tiled hall without further protest.

Sorcha followed along behind them, twisted in confusion. She was back in her proper timeline, wasn't she? Then how had Jonathan known about Hew? And why had he made those comments before in the well about her not being where she wanted to be?"

The crowd parted for Jonathan as he moved through the kitchen and into the small side room. The room that only a short while ago - or was it a lifetime ago? – had served as her changing room. But there was no washing station set up in this version of the room. The bed lay neat and untouched; there were no piles of ragged, blood-stained clothes discarded in a corner.

Sorcha hurried to prop up several pillows at the head of the bed, and then Jonathan carefully lay Hew down against them. The man wrapped his arms around his chest, drawing his knees in close, looking nervously around at the group.

He was in even worse shape than Sorcha had realized. His shirt was in tatters and she could see his ribs pressing through his skin. His pants' original color could barely be seen through the thick layers of grime.

Biddy strode in with a tray holding a bowl of stew, a spoon, and a large cup of wine. She lay it down across Hew's lap. "There you go, duck. You dig on in. There's more where that came from." Shen she turned to smile fondly at Jonathan. She murmured, "The shirt off his own back, he would." Then she turned to shoo away the many curious eyes that peered into the room. "Enough, enough," she scolded them. "Let the man eat in peace."

Hew looked between Jonathan and Sorcha in bewilderment. His eyes moved to the food, and she could see the war in them between soul-deep hunger and gripping fear.

She knelt down at his side. "It's not a trick, Hew. Go on, take a bite."

He hesitated, then at last hunger won out. His shaking hand reached forward, took up the spoon, and carefully scooped up some of the stew. He put it in his mouth, and a groan of bliss emanated from his entire being. And then he began eating as if he hadn't had a decent meal in a year.

Jonathan was still staring down at Hew as if the man were a ghost. At last he drew a chair over to Hew's side, sat in it, and tenderly rested a hand on Hew's shoulder. Hew shuddered, as if he had been hit, but then he relaxed again and continued to eat.

Sorcha drew her eyes up to Jonathan's. "I don't understand. Do you know Hew?"

Jonathan's voice was rough. "Yes. Well, no. I have dreamt about him often."

Understanding began to dawn in Sorcha's mind. "You've been dreaming about what life might have been like, ever since Florie's accident."

He somberly nodded. "It seemed so real. The desolation it caused to my family. The life I was forced to lead. The streets weren't kind to me." He nudged his head at the withered man before them. "Hew stood by me. Through it all, Hew was what kept me alive." He gave a wry smile. "Well, kept *him* alive. The Jonathan I would have been."

Sorcha looked at Jonathan. "And the other Jonathan, he said he would have dreams about what Florie would have been like. He must have been seeing your world?"

Jonathan's gaze moved to the man before him. "I have taken so much for granted, all these years," he murmured. "I had so much, and it could have all been gone, in the mere blink of an eye. A mere few seconds later. That is what Jonathan – the other version of me – has had to live with for his entire life."

His eyes turned to Sorcha, and they held powerful emotions that she could not even begin to name. "And now I've taken you away from him."

Sorcha's voice caught in her throat. She finally found breath. "You saw us?"

His voice was rough. "When I fell in the well, I'm not sure what happened. It seemed like a dream, but it felt quite real. I saw it all. From when you woke up alongside those kittens, to discovering the saddle, to challenging Julia and Felton in the main room."

His gaze shadowed. "I saw how much you risked for him. I watched your agony over your final choice to come back in the well. To come back to your own time." His jaw tightened. "To leave him behind."

Sorcha twined her fingers into his, looking up into those amber eyes, now full of pain and longing.

"Oh, Jonathan, he *is* you," she vowed. "And you are him. He is not alone. He has the other me – and they will love each other like no other couple on Earth ever could."

She flushed, but she held his gaze. "Well, like almost no other couple."

He groaned, then pulled her up. They were in each other's arms, kissing each other, and the world around them ceased to exist. There was him, and her, and together they filled the universe.

Chapter 5

Hew had finished his second bowl of stew
and was now snoring peacefully beneath a thick
blanket. Sorcha wondered if it was the first time
he had been at ease in the past decade. She gently
closed the door on the room, then stepped out to
take a seat by the box of kittens. She looked down
into it, selecting up the black one with its white
blaze.

She looked at him in curiosity. "I wonder who
did rescue the kittens, in the other timeline, if it
wasn't you."

Jonathan brought over a cup of wine, shaking
his head. "The legends about that well are
fractured and contradictory. I had never thought
them true, of course." He gave a wry smile. "Until
you came along."

He looked over at the closed door. "Take
Hew. Out of all the doorsteps he could have
chosen to sleep on tonight, he landed on ours? I

think the tear in time that Julia caused is like an open wound. It keeps trying to heal. But the rent is too large to do it evenly, so it ends up jagged and tossed."

He looked back down into the box. "Somehow, the mother cat was still slain. And somehow, these wee kittens still made their way here. Maybe, in the other timeline, it was one of the maids who gathered them up."

Sorcha gave a small smile. "I suppose we'll never know, unless we can find a way to send letters through the well."

His brow creased. "Don't even think about using that well again. It's sheer luck you made it through that alive. Most tales about the well end with heartache and sorrow. Someone tries to use it to change something, and the results are far worse than the original outcome."

Sorcha twined her fingers into his. "I won't use it, I promise."

His eyes shadowed. "Even though the other Jonathan is on the other side?"

She leant forward to run her fingers through his hair. "I have my own Jonathan, right here with me."

His eyes eased into hers, deep, without measure.

Biddy poked her head in from the hallway. "I've held them off as much as I could, ducks, but the guests are growing restless. I think one of you should come out and say something before they begin to riot."

Jonathan looked back toward the main room, and his gaze hardened. "Julia is in there. And Felton."

"But she didn't kill your sister, not here," Sorcha gently reminded him. "She hasn't been living with the torments of guilt for ten long years. If we showed her the saddle and the blanket, she'd laugh it off, or say someone must have made an innocent mistake." She glanced toward the garden. "And with the incident seeming a dangerous but normal accident with no real harm done, did your mother bury the horse in the back yard?"

Jonathan shook his head. "No. We simply had a horse butcher come to the stables and pick Speckles up. I have no idea where they took her body."

Sorcha nodded. "So we have no real crime and no proof. Julia failed in that attempt, so she married her older sister off to a middle-aged man who lives far away. That can hardly be something we take her to task for. And now, if she is pursuing both you and Felton at the same time, that might be immoral, but it's not quite illegal."

Jonathan's brow darkened. "She killed my sister. I've seen it in my dreams, a thousand times. I saw what it did to our family."

He glanced again at the other room. "She had something to do with it, whichever time she's in," he stated. "She knew about the well. She threw you into it, to get you out of the way. Who knows what other harm she's caused? What new evils she might she do in the future?"

Sorcha found she agreed with him. "So what are we going to do?"

His lips pressed together in resolution. "I'm going to use myself as bait."

Sorcha instantly shook her head. "Oh, no you don't! I almost lost you just now, and things are finally getting back to normal. I can't risk losing you again!"

"I'll be careful," he promised. "But you said it yourself, when talking to … Johnny." A wry smile came to his lips. "Having two Jonathans is going to get a bit confusing. But you had said to Johnny that you thought she was thinking of killing me, once she was assured of gaining the Ladyship."

Sorcha nodded. "She definitely seems to be scheming with Felton. He wants the Lordship, and she wants it all. So I think she's been wooing you as a backup plan, but ideally they would get you out of the way so they can have the house and money all to themselves."

"So we give them the opportunity," he agreed. "But not here. My parents have been through too much. Her sister, Theodoria, is planning on returning home with Percy tomorrow. They live in Dover. Julia's been after me for months to take a trip down there with her. So I think her and Felton's plan must involve that trip or destination."

He smiled at Sorcha. "It seems I simply have to agree to go along with her to Dover. I'll catch her in the act, and then we have all the proof we need."

Sorcha crossed her arms in front of her chest. "If you're going, then I'm going, too."

His brow narrowed. "This is going to be dangerous."

"Exactly my point," she retorted. "You're going to need someone to watch your back. And, besides, I've seen her from another angle. I could spot things you might miss."

His frown deepened. "If Julia thinks I'm giving in to her courtships, how are we possibly going to explain that you're coming along for the ride? The last thing she'll want is a potential competitor to be on this trip."

Sorcha gave it some thought. "I imagine I've been acting quite bizarrely these past few hours, as my other-me came to grips with this new world she had been thrust into." Her eyes lit up. "You can tell her that you've realized I was in shock, because my mother has been abusing me all this time."

His eyes darkened. "They'd definitely believe that last part."

She waved a hand in the air. "Reassure Julia that you have no interest in me other than as an innocent victim who needs help. You could suggest that I go down to rest with Theodoria and her husband for several months, to let the sea soothe me. I'm sure Julia would be thrilled with the idea of me and Theodoria sitting, staring at the sea, for hours on end. And that would give her free rein to map out whatever scheme she has involving you."

Jonathan shook his head. "Sorcha, I'm not sure that –"

Sorcha leant forward. "Either you do that, or I'll tell them all every last detail. And whether they think I'm loony or not, Julia could high-tail it for France. You'll never bring her to justice – but you'll be safe."

Jonathan gave a low laugh. "You certainly have changed from when I first met you."

Sorcha's eyes shone. "I have something to live for, now."

He twined his fingers into her. "As do I."

He let out a long breath. "All right. We'll do it your way. But you be careful, too. I can't lose you."

She smiled. "Careful as a mouse."

Chapter 6

Sorcha knew her role, and she shuffled, eyes down, behind Jonathan as he guided her through the throngs into the center of the main room. Warm relief swept over her as she saw the two paintings of Jonathan and Florie hanging in their proper locations over the mantle. For the thousandth time Sorcha thought of how much had been changed because of one short split-second timing.

She wondered how many other aspects of life hung by a thread – how many precious moments acted as a make-or-break life-changing incident for a person. For example, if her mother had not gotten sick at that Christmas party, so many years ago, would she have been sent off to marry a Scotsman who would abandon her? Would she have hardened into the miserable, abusive woman she had become?

Sorcha shook her head. Whatever fate had laid on Madeline's shoulders, Madeline still had a choice of how to face that prospect. There was always a way.

Jonathan held up his hands, drawing the murmuring conversation around them into silence. "Ladies and gentlemen, I'm sure you have many questions about what had happened here tonight. Let me set your mind at ease. Both Sorcha and I are all right. It seems she stumbled, in the darkness, and fell down an old well we have in our gardens. But I went down to fetch her out, and we are both fine now."

A flutter of relieved sighs circled the room.

He smiled at the guests. "So please, go on enjoying our party. I am so grateful to each and every one of you for being here to celebrate my birthday with me." His gaze warmed with emotion. "It means more to me than you could possibly know."

Applause filled the room, and he waved his thanks before gently escorting Sorcha out again. In a few moments they had crossed the hallway's black-and-white tiles and found the relative quiet of the library.

Sorcha's eyes went to the red binding of the book of Robert Burns's poetry, and she drew in a breath. How much she owed to that poet and his works.

There was motion behind them and Lord and Lady Davenport entered the room, followed by Julia. All three looked to Sorcha with sympathy – although Sorcha only believed the intention behind two of those gazes.

Lady Davenport took her hand. "My child, are you sure you're all right? You've been through quite a lot tonight."

Jonathan held his mother's gaze. "Mother, I think she might be in shock. You saw how she was acting earlier this evening. I have the sense that …" He dropped his tone into a rough whisper. "… that her mother might be abusive."

Lady Davenport's eyes shadowed. "I always worried about that. Madeline's mother was a hard woman who believed in the power of the rod to cure a child. When Madeline was sent so far away I thought it a blessing in disguise. Madeline could finally be free of her mother and start a fresh life, one full of joy and laughter."

Her eyes dropped. "It seems fate was not kind to her."

Jonathan nodded. "Indeed, although Madeline herself bears the responsibility for what she has done to Sorcha all these years. I'm afraid tonight might have been the final straw for Sorcha's tender mind."

Julia's eyes shone with delight, but she drew a concerned pout to her lips.

Jonathan drew his gaze across the three others in the room. "Whatever her mother did or threatened, Sorcha seems almost in shock. I'm worried that she could take months to heal, if she ever does."

Lady Davenport waved a hand back toward her home. "Why, of course, she should stay here, with us. For as long as it takes."

Jonathan's brow creased. "I'm not sure if having her stay here is the best idea. This long night in these surroundings is what pushed her over the edge. If she were trapped here for weeks on end, Sorcha might just relive those agonies over and over again."

He sighed. "If only there were somewhere else we could take her. Somewhere far away – as far from Scotland and her mother as possible. Somewhere quiet where she could simply stare at the rolling sea for long hours on end. I think that might help her to find some sort of peace."

Julia's eyes lit up with interest. "Why, Jonathan! I've been asking you for months to come with me to Dover. My sister's husband has a home there! I'm sure that would be perfect for Sorcha. We could set her up with a chair on the beach. She could stare at the waves from sunrise to sunset."

Jonathan turned to her, his face holding cautious hope. "Are you sure your sister wouldn't mind? After all, I doubt Sorcha would be an engaging houseguest. My guess is she'll just remain in that chair for hours on end, doing nothing at all."

Sorcha did her best to stare vacantly at the ground, acting the part.

Julia's smile grew wider, and she eagerly nodded. "Absolutely. That sounds perfect. And it's just the excuse for you to come down with us, to make sure we get there safely. After all, you wouldn't want anything to happen to us during that long trip, would you?"

His eyes shone. "I would not. You are too kind to make the offer."

A predatory grin sparkled on her face. "It will be my pleasure."

Lady Davenport looked between the two. "Well, then, it seems settled. When do you think you'll want to head out?"

Julia promptly spoke up. "If we truly care for Sorcha, we should head out immediately. We should not delay one moment longer." She drew on a gaze of concern. "After all, this poor duck has been traumatized enough. We should start her healing as soon as possible. I'm sure all five us can fit into my sister's carriage."

Jonathan gave a small smile. "I would prefer to ride alongside, on my own horse. That way you and Sorcha can sleep in comfort on the bench opposite the couple."

Julia nodded absently in agreement. She looked over Sorcha with growing pleasure. "I am sure if we sit Sorcha in front of the sea for a few months that she will find the peace she seeks." Her eyes flitted up to hold Jonathan's. "And you and I could spend some time together."

Lady Davenport looked at Jonathan. "Are you sure you want to leave immediately? It'll be a long ride for you, to take on horseback. And you haven't slept all night."

Jonathan nodded. "We should leave now. Julia's right. It is best for Sorcha that we remove her from anything which might trigger her harsh memories."

Lady Davenport smiled. "You are always such an understanding soul, Jonathan. First Hew, and now Sorcha. I am so proud of the man you have grown into."

Jonathan's eyes shone, and he stepped forward to give her a hug. It was a long moment before they separated again.

Lady Davenport nodded to her husband. "Well, then, it seems the party will be losing its guest of honor sooner than we had expected." She turned to call out into the hallway, "Biddy?"

Sorcha imagined that Biddy had been lurking right around the corner listening in on the conversation, because the woman appeared as if by magic. "Yes, M'Lady?"

"Please help Sorcha here up into the lavender guest room so she can bathe. While she does, coordinate with the maids to pack up a trunk for her. She'll be leaving shortly on an extended trip to Dover."

"As you wish, M'Lady," agreed Biddy. She looked to Jonathan, her eyes twinkling, and then she stepped past him. "Come right with me, lass. We'll get everything right as rain for you."

Jonathan looked down at Sorcha. "I will see you soon. Everything will be all right. Trust in me."

It took all her strength not to look up at him, not to lose herself in those warm, amber eyes. She nodded, moving past him and following Biddy up the stairs.

She didn't realize how wholly exhausted she was until she stepped into the beautifully appointed bedroom. It took all her strength to stay awake while the tub was brought up and filled. By the time she slipped into the rose-scented bath, the yawns were coming fast and furious. But she knew she couldn't linger. If she was tired, Jonathan was undoubtedly even more worn out, given all he had learned about his family. She owed it to him to get this process into motion.

In short order she was dressed in traveling clothes and stepping into the kitchens. Jonathan was in there with Biddy, packing apples and wine into a basket.

Sorcha looked around the kitchen, then stepped forward to Jonathan. She kept her voice low. "Are you sure we shouldn't wait until tomorrow to head down to Dover? I'll get to ride in the carriage, but you'll be on horseback. You must be exhausted already!"

He shook his head, keeping his voice quiet as well. "I'll be all right. I don't want that snake in our house one more second than necessary." He glanced toward the main hallway. "I want her as far away as possible from my sister and my parents."

Biddy came over with a concerned look in her eye, tucking another bottle of wine into the basket. "I don't know what you two are up to, but you both be careful," she scolded. "In shock, my foot. This woman is as sharp as a tack."

Sorcha smiled fondly at her, giving her a hug. "We'll be fine," she soothed the older woman. "You just take care of those little kittens. I expect to find eight happy, healthy little cats when I return."

Jonathan turned. "And about Hew," he added. "Please treat that man like my best friend." His gaze gentled. "He deserves it."

Biddy smiled. "Done, and done." Her face warmed. "And you, my Johnny, you take care of yourself."

He gently wrapped his arms around her, holding her for a long moment. His voice was rough in her ear. "Ah, Biddy. You always believed in me."

She held him tenderly. "And I always shall." Then she drew back, wiping at her eyes. "Now, off with you two. Get whatever it is you're up to done with, and then come back home, safe and sound."

He gave her a wink. "As you wish."

It seemed the blink of an eye before Theodoria, Percy, Julia, and Sorcha were ensconced in the carriage and rumbling along the road toward Dover.

Theodoria was snoring gently, curled up against her husband, who was also sound asleep. Julia gazed at them in contemplation for a few minutes. Then she turned to Sorcha.

"So, tell me, Sorcha. What did I look like?"

Chapter 7

Sorcha blinked in shock. Had Julia guessed what she and Jonathan were up to?

Sorcha strove to keep her features neutral. "I'm sorry, Julia, I think I'm confused. What you looked like? When? During the party this evening?"

Julia stretched back against the leather seat, a contented smile stretching on her lips. "In the other, alternate time stream. The one where Felton and I have already achieved the success I crave so much."

Sorcha's breath caught in her throat. "I don't know what you mean."

Julia gave a barking laugh. "You were only over there for a few hours, so clearly you found a way to hop back into the well before the portal closed. I give you points for thinking quickly." Her grin grew. "And it's not like you can tell anybody what happened and have them believe you. The gateway's now closed, of course, so you can't prove that passageway exists."

Her eyes lit up. "So there's only me you can talk to about it."

You and Jonathan.

Sorcha kept her face as still as possible. She didn't want to do anything to derail Jonathan's plans. She added a tenuous tone to her voice. "I'm not sure what happened. It was all very … very confusing."

Julia chuckled. "Jonathan was right to say you've been through a shock." Satisfaction shone in her gaze. "And whatever it was Jonathan thought he saw in you before, he certainly had his mind set straight by your erratic behavior these past few hours."

She nodded in self-assurance. "It's fairly clear, from the things he was saying to me while you got ready, that he finally sees that you're not up to his level. You've lost your chance completely, girl, and it will never come again."

It took every ounce of self-control for Sorcha to maintain her calm, vapid stare. What the woman needed was a good punch in the face. For starters.

She added incredulity to her tone. "I don't know what you mean, Julia. How could I possibly ever be at Jonathan's level?"

"So true," agreed Julia with a contented smile. "So absolutely true. You just enjoy your long, quiet recuperation with my sister. You two will be absolutely perfect for each other."

Julia leant forward, and her eyes lit up with interest. "But back to your little adventure in time. You were there. You saw her. You actually *saw* her. The woman I so long to be."

Her face shone with rapt attention. "Tell me, what was her dress like?"

Sorcha fought to keep the grin off her face. She had thought Julia would be worried about any knowledge Sorcha had learned. Perhaps details about Julia's nefarious deeds. Hidden issues that might help Sorcha cause trouble for the Julia in this life.

Instead, apparently Julia only cared about hearing soaring tales of her own success and beauty.

Sorcha made her eyes round with wonder. "Oh, you were a stunning goddess, Julia" she extolled. "You were by far the most beautiful woman in the room. Felton was completely absorbed by you."

Julia beamed. "Yes, yes, tell me more."

"Your dress was layers of ivory muslin and silk," continued Sorcha. "The most beautiful embroidery of rosettes streamed down its length. Larger rosettes gathered around the bottom, along with golden scallops."

Julia brought her hands to her chest in bliss. "It sounds gorgeous."

Sorcha nodded. "And the necklace. Moonstone and pearl, sapphire and peridot. The largest I had ever seen. I truly believe it belonged in a museum."

Julia's lips drew together. "And that hideous plateware the Davenports always had on display?"

Sorcha shook her head. "I think you and Felton had already shipped it off to an auction house, or something like that. You were preparing for your wedding."

A delighted sigh escaped from Julia's lips. "Perfect. Absolutely perfect. Everything is going just as planned."

Her gaze hardened, and she leaned forward. "I know this is all confusing to you, so I'll try to keep it simple. Time tries to find a balance. If you try to change things here, time will just find a way to sort it back to the way it was meant to be. So don't try to interfere with me and Felton having it all. It just wouldn't work."

"Of course," agreed Sorcha quietly. "You and Felton deserve each other."

"That we do," Julia agreed with delight. "And soon, very soon, we will get all that is coming to us."

Sorcha's eyes glowed with determination. "I will pray for that with all my soul."

Julia patted her on the knee. "Good lass. Now get some sleep. You've had a long day." She laughed. "Or long multiple days."

Sorcha nodded and curled back up against the opposite corner.

She would want to have all her wits about her for whatever was to come ahead.

Chapter 8

The carriage jolted to a stop, and Sorcha blinked her eyes open. The group had taken breaks several times through their journey, as daylight cycled through its normal arc, but now it was once again dark outside. The rough bustle seemed to indicate they had finally reached London proper – the midway point of their journey.

Julia looked around with delighted glee. "We're here! And we're just in time."

Sorcha rubbed her eyes in confusion. "In time for what?"

"Why, for the ball, of course!" Julia cried, looking at Sorcha as if she were daft. Which, of course, for all intents and purposes, Sorcha was supposed to be. So Sorcha did her part and let her mouth hang open like an *eejit*.

Sorcha shook her head. "Of course you wouldn't know about Almack's. I bet you hold dances in a cow barn." Her eyes glowed. "But for tonight, you'll see what real culture is about. Almack's Assembly Rooms. Only the best of the best get in there, and now we have Jonathan with us. He'll get us entrance." Her eyes sharpened. "At least until we don't need him any more."

Sorcha made a show of looking down her outfit. The household of the Davenports had made sure she was freshly cleaned and dressed before she left on the trip, but she certainly didn't have anything ball-worthy in her luggage. Just simple traveling clothes.

Julia waved a hand. "Oh, don't worry about that. We'll stop down at Bond Street and get something perfectly suitable."

Sorcha looked out the window at the fading sunset. "But it's long past –"

Julia was already leaning out her side window. "Oh, Jonathan! Jonathan, darling!"

Sorcha could see he was handing his horse off to a groom, and then he came over. He nodded to the two women. "The inn-keep can have our dinner ready in about a half hour, if –"

Julia waved a hand. "Oh, none of that! We're going to Almack's!"

Jonathan looked between Julia and Sorcha. "We are?"

"But of course," she insisted. "I absolutely am dying to go. And of course both Sorcha and I must have new clothes to prepare for this."

Sorcha kept her lips closed. She had no idea why Julia wanted her along, but there was no way she would let Julia out alone with Jonathan.

Jonathan's eyes slid to the sleeping couple across from the two women. "What about your sister?"

Julia laughed. "Thea will want to be in bed by nine," she responded. "The inn staff will get them settled with some boiled roast and a large bed. They'll be happy as pigs in slop."

Sorcha could see the curiosity in Jonathan's gaze, but his face remained even. "Of course, if that is what you'd like," he agreed. "Shall I come along to help you shop?"

"Oh, no," insisted Julia. "That would ruin the surprise. We'll be back in no time, don't you worry."

Jonathan's gaze creased further, but after a moment he nodded. "I look forward to it."

His gaze swept to Sorcha, and she held her breath. The connection between them was palpable – a visceral force which could never be severed.

And then he stepped away.

In a moment the other two occupants of the coach had disembarked, the door had been closed again, and the coach was on its way. It was only a few minutes before it was pulling up along the most elegant sets of shops Sorcha had ever seen.

Julia's eyes glowed with delight. Her murmur was almost reverential. "And this is where it all begins. This is where her world and mine finally merge together – where all that has been wrong these past years is finally, irrevocably, set to rights."

She eyed the line of shop options carefully before settling on a building which seemed to have gold leaf gilding every corner and knob. "That one."

She strode up to it and pushed open the door. Only one other patron was inside – an elderly woman with rows of pearls dangling against her breast. Shelves lined the walls, holding a collection of fabrics too beautiful to contemplate. Other cases held buttons and stays of intricate complexity.

A tall, slender man in a grey suit approached Julia. "And how might I help you two lovely ladies this evening? Are you planning outfits for the Christmas season?"

Julia's gaze shone with determination. "We both need new dresses for tonight's ball at Almack's."

He blinked at her like an owl, his eyes round and startled. "Oh, but miss, that would be –"

Julia stepped forward. "We are with the party of Jonathan Davenport, and nothing – I repeat *nothing* – is going to prevent us from attending. Money is no cost. Call up every seamstress that you know and pay them whatever they demand. For we *will* be there tonight."

The man's eyes lit up like pound coins. He turned to the back room and called out, "Boys!"

A trio of young lads, smartly dressed, tumbled into the room, and in a moment a whirlwind had begun.

Seamstresses were summoned. Then more. Julia pulled out and discarded cloth after cloth, peppering Sorcha for precise details about the "other" Julia's apparel. It seemed Julia wanted to out-do her alter ego, to win this race that the two were currently running neck-and-neck.

Sorcha held in a grin as Julia sent one seamstress off with the under-linens and another with the upper layer. Julia hadn't realized that the woman she was competing with was undoubtedly, at this very moment, under lock and key, awaiting trial for double homicide. With any luck, this current version of the woman would soon be reduced to the same level.

Julia was gracious, choosing out an admirable set of colors for Sorcha – ivory silk with a pale blue over-layer. The colors set off Sorcha's red hair, and even she had to admit she looked stunning in the combination as she looked in the mirror.

Sorcha had a sense that Julia did it out of self-preservation. Julia wouldn't want to be seen in the company of anyone less than perfect, on her first night out in her new form. Also, Julia seemed to want Sorcha to continually reassure her that she was, indeed, now out-doing her alter ego.

The army of seamstresses got to work. They coordinated in teams to cut, stitch, and hold up fabric to examine its seams. Like a well-honed militia they worked at lightning speed to meet their deadline.

Time spun on in clipping of shears and movements of needles.

Julia huddled over her dress, eagerly engaging the seamstress in an intense discussion about the finer distinctions of roses versus curling spirals. Sorcha took the opportunity to move to the large front window to look out. The moonlit streets were swathed in shimmering silver; foot traffic was changing into evening gowns and black wear for the men. Apparently half of London had decided it was the perfect night to explore the theater or opera.

Sorcha's gaze moved across the street - and she stopped.

Jonathan was standing against the opposite corner, his gaze shadowed, his attention clearly on the shop. His shoulders eased when he saw Sorcha, and he nodded.

Sorcha smiled, nodding back. It warmed her heart that he was keeping an eye on her. But, at least for now, he needn't have bothered. Julia was a woman on a mission, and Sorcha felt sorry for any seamstress who tried to step between her and her evening of triumph.

Julia gave a call. "Sorcha! Stop your daydreaming! Come over here and try on your new dress."

Sorcha's eyes shone with the thought of how close Julia was to her just rewards. And then Sorcha tempered her features, took in a breath, and meekly turned to do Julia's bidding.

Chapter 9

Sorcha's heart thumped in nervous anticipation as she adjusted her necklace before her mirror in the inn's room. Julia had insisted the two women have separate rooms, and Jonathan had agreed without question. Indeed, Sorcha thought he might have been concerned with the thought of the viper having access to her all night long without any witnesses about.

Sorcha knew tonight was just for show – she doubted Julia would cause any harm to Jonathan when her grand entrance was being made. And yet, a thrill ran through her as she swept her hand down the beautiful teal fabric. The dress, truly, was stunning. She wondered how much Jonathan would be in debt for this.

A loud knock sounded on her door; Julia's voice sung through it. "C'mon, Sorcha, or we'll leave without you!"

Sorcha highly doubted that Jonathan would do any such thing, but she didn't want to cause any disturbance in the flow of events. She called out, meekly, "I'll be right there."

A last tuck of her curls into her updo, and she was ready.

Jonathan and Julia were talking at the bottom of the stairs as she descended, and both turned to look at her. Julia's face beamed with satisfaction – with the smirk that she had managed to turn a sow's ear into a silk purse. But Jonathan's gaze held something deeper – something richer. She could see the struggle it took him to press that emotion back down into a look of casual acceptance.

He nodded to Julia and put out an arm. "And at last we have our chaperone. Shall we be off?"

Julia's eyes shone. "We shall indeed."

A short ride in a carriage, a short wait in the disembarkation line, and they were stepping into the storied halls of Almack's Assembly Rooms. The ballroom was stunning, with a row of tall, arched windows and glass mirrors which made the room seem to go on forever. A band in a corner was playing a reel, dancers were on the floor, and laughter filled the room.

For a moment all the machinations and worries of the past days drifted away. Sorcha had never been at a dance, certainly not one like this, and absolutely never dressed the way she was. Sorcha could see a number of the men and women looking her way, casting appreciative glances. Her instinct was to shy away, to watch for her mother's reaction. But her mother wasn't here. Sorcha was free of her.

The thought still staggered her.

Jonathan was standing between Julia and Sorcha, nodding at something Julia said to him, but Sorcha had the sense that he took in every look, every movement around the room. And when he suddenly stiffened, Sorcha instantly followed his gaze.

Felton was walking toward them.

Felton's eyes lit up with delight. "Ah, Jonathan, I didn't realize you'd be here! What a pleasant surprise." He turned to Julia. "And Julia! Looking more beautiful than ever. What an extraordinary treat."

The music came to a stop, and applause filled the air. Felton put an arm out to Julia. "Perhaps you might join me for the next set?"

She fluttered her eyes up to Jonathan. "Only if Jonathan allows it, of course."

He gave a smile. "By all means, enjoy yourself. It's why we're here."

The two merged off into the crowd, their heads close together.

Jonathan turned to Sorcha and put out his hand. His look shimmered, deepened, and her breath caught.

His voice was hoarse. "May I have the honor?"

She could only nod.

She knew in a distant corner of her mind that Julia and Felton were on the other side of the room, undoubtedly at this very moment plotting Jonathan's demise. But she didn't care. For a brief, shining, glorious pause she was dancing with Jonathan. They were turning, whirling in abandon.

He was hers.

He was taking her hand, he was smiling down at her, they were moving back to back. They matched and flowed like she never had thought possible.

She turned and put out her hand to the next person in line –

Her mother stared at her, aghast, looking down her outfit as if the very gates of Hell had opened up. Her voice dripped fury.

"Sorcha! What on Earth are you doing here?"

Chapter 10

Sorcha could barely breathe. It was as if every nightmare had come to life. Her mother's hand snaked out, heading for her wrist –

Jonathan stepped forward, his body smoothly blocking the grab. "What a surprise to find you here, Mrs. McClintock. And I see you are not alone. Hello, Mr. Denton."

Sorcha blinked in surprise. It was the tall lawyer with piercing blue eyes from the Davenport's house. The man her mother had made a bee-line for after Lord Davenport's speech. The man she now suspected had been her mother's childhood beau.

The lawyer put a hand possessively on Madeline's shoulder. "It is good to see you again, Master Davenport."

Madeline flushed, looking nervously between Mr. Denton and Sorcha.

Jonathan stepped to the side, bringing Sorcha into the group. "Mr. Denton, I'm not sure that you've met. Let me introduce to you Miss Sorcha McClintock, Madeline's daughter."

Mr. Denton blinked in surprise, but then recovered and put his hand out to Sorcha. She automatically placed hers in his and waited while he lowered his head to a kiss.

His eyes drew down her form. "Sorcha, you are indeed the loveliest woman at this ball tonight."

Madeline's eyes narrowed, but she bit her lip, saying nothing.

Mr. Denton continued to focus on Sorcha. "Your mother was quite a beauty when she was younger, but of course her parents married her off to that Laird's son with the wealth and lands. Noble heritage and all of that. I ran into her again, maybe eight years back, and I was delighted to remake her acquaintance."

He looked warmly down at Sorcha. "So now I must content myself with visiting whenever I'm up on business in the north." He raised an eyebrow. "It's a shame that I've never run into you before. Funny that the timing just never worked out."

Sorcha's heart hammered against her ribs. Funny, indeed. She had no doubt that her mother's sudden desire to have her spend the day helping a sick neighbor or walking ten miles to fetch some herbs had something to do with these visits.

Mr. Denton looked to Madeline, and his gaze shadowed. "Some say wealth is a blessing. However, it also often comes with its burdens. It can require one to do what one's parents instruct, right or wrong."

Jonathan's arm wrapped around Sorcha's side, giving her waist a gentle squeeze. His voice was calm. "Not always."

Madeline's gaze could have shredded granite, but her lips moved into a smile. "Come, Mr. Denton, I find that I am feeling hungry. Let's see what is available in the next room."

Mr. Denton smiled warmly at Jonathan and Sorcha. "I hope that we shall see each other around." Then he guided Madeline around the corner.

Sorcha could not take her eyes off the shadows where her mother had just vanished. The thought slowly fermented in her head, gaining traction with every passing moment.

Had her mother been seeing this old boyfriend of hers? While her father was away?

Jonathan followed the direction of her gaze. His tone was tender but firm. "As much as your mother is at fault here, I have a feeling that your father is not much different – if, perhaps, a bit more discreet."

A week ago Sorcha would have fought the accusation with every ounce of her strength. But with all she had been through, with all she had learned, she could only nod.

She lowered her gaze.

Jonathan ran a hand down her hair. "Life isn't always easy," he pointed out. "Especially when you are trapped with someone you don't love."

He sighed. "I'm not saying their behavior is honorable. And I absolutely do not agree with your mother becoming abusive. But I imagine their lives might have been far different, if just one brief moment in time had changed. If both had simply been allowed by fate to follow their hearts."

Sorcha twined her fingers into his. "The twists of fate have brought you to me, and for that I thank them, despite all else that it entailed."

She blushed, but she said the words which echoed so strongly in her heart. "I know, no matter what life has in store for me, that, once vowed, I would never stray. If I were to pledge myself to a man, it would be fully and wholly."

She looked up at him.

If only the fates would be so kind ...

His gaze shone as he read the unspoken thoughts behind her eyes.

His voice was a low murmur. "I, too, would be true. Fully and wholly."

Time shimmered and wrapped them.

At last he gave a soft smile, nodding to her. "Many in the world are not as fortunate as we are. When we choose, we will be able to choose for love." His voice grew hoarse. "For those are the vows that will last a lifetime."

She gave a smile which reached to her soul.

"Several lifetimes."

Chapter 11

Sorcha lolled pleasantly against her leather bench as the carriage bobbed its way to Dover. Once she had come to terms with the presence of her mother at the ball, the evening had been exquisite. Her mother had made a pointed effort to avoid being in the same room with her, and she saw the fondness with which Mr. Denton gazed at her mother the times the two were together.

She wondered just how her mother might have turned out if she hadn't spent years abandoned in a loveless marriage with a man who, Sorcha could now see, was probably leaving her for other woman every chance he got. Maybe the cruel streak created by Madeline's brutal childhood would never have honed so sharply, exacerbated by long, lonely nights and a future which stretched into oblivion.

She shook her head. It still did not excuse all her mother had done – and Sorcha would never again return to that home. Her mother would have to find another path toward regaining a sense of meaning.

Julia was humming the melody of one of the reels to herself, her hands swaying to and fro. She looked across at the sleeping couple across from them and then turned to Sorcha. Her voice was surprisingly mild, almost curious. "I saw your mother there, at the ball last night. I saw you talking with her."

Sorcha flushed. She wasn't sure what the proper response might be, so she simply nodded.

Julia looked back at her hands. "You should count yourself lucky, to be able to spend time with your mother. To know what she's like."

Sorcha's brow creased in confusion. "But you seem to spend lots of time with Lydia."

Julia snorted. "Lydia. That fat cow isn't my mother. The only reason she adopted me and sleeping beauty here is that our blonde hair matched hers."

Sorcha shook her head. "I didn't realize you were adopted."

Julia grinned. "Hardly anybody does. My mother tried everything with my father, but he was weak and apparently impotent. They came out from London to Bath to *visit the healing waters*, or so they told everyone. Stayed for a number of months and, voila, returned with my sister. A few years later they acquired me."

Sorcha was intrigued by this. Did this mean Julia and Thea weren't really sisters? It might explain better how Julia had been so ruthless in her plans to get rid of her elder sibling. She leant forward. "So who *was* your mother?"

Julia's eyes sparkled. "Ah, here's where it gets interesting. Apparently my mother was a talented witch with quite a reputation. Love potions, fertility spells, that sort of thing. But her own husband was a nasty lout. Kept her under his thumb. And, no matter what she tried, he never gave her a child."

Her eyes glowed. "And then she heard about the well."

Sorcha could barely breathe.

Julia nodded. "She saw her way out. She waited until the passageway was open, and then she entered the other world. She danced, drank, and courted every man she'd ever lusted after." Her gaze moved to Theodoria. "When my mother returned from her night of celebration, she was pregnant."

Sorcha's eyes went round. "Isn't that dangerous?"

Julia barked with laughter. "As if my mother cared. She figured the rift would heal soon enough – sending one life through, bringing two back. And it worked so well that she went through a few more times. The last time, I came back with her."

Sorcha looked at her in wonder. "So who is your father?"

Julia shrugged. "I don't know. I don't think my mother even knew. She wanted to maximize her chances of getting pregnant. I don't think she cared just who it was. As long as it worked."

"But surely you could ask her if –"

Julia shook her head. "There's a risk, you know, if you're not careful. My mother was doing all of these outrageous acts and then sending her other version back to face the consequences. My mother wasn't smart about it. Not discreet. So then, one time, when I was maybe four, she just never came back again."

Sorcha's throat closed up. "Maybe she was killed by a highwayman or something else equally awful happened to her."

Julia's teeth gleamed. "My bet is that the other version of my mother ended up murdered by her husband for 'what she had done.' That is, what my mother had done in her name."

Julia's gaze darkened. "And then when my mother attempted to go through the well, to change places as it were with the dead woman, she ended up trapped in a grave and smothered to death herself."

A smile quirked. "Or maybe she did go through, even though the other woman was dead. When she was seen, she was thought to be an evil spirit, and was killed as well."

"You don't even know?"

Julia shrugged. "It doesn't matter. All I know is my father went off in a drunken rage when she didn't return and got himself killed in a bar fight. Next thing I know, this strange blonde woman is looking to take us in – first Thea, then me. She instructed us to call her 'Mama.' "

She grinned. "And so we did."

Sorcha thought of sweet Lydia, with her warm smile, and these two children she thought of as innocent orphans.

Sorcha looked over at Theodoria, resting against her husband. Maybe that explained why the poor woman had ended up the way she had. She had made that time-transition while still in the womb. And perhaps it explained some of Julia's issues as well.

She turned to Julia. "Have you ever been through the well yourself?"

Julia shook her head. "I learned my lesson from my mother. It's too dangerous. You never know what awaits you on the other side." She nodded her head at Sorcha. "But it didn't work out so badly for you, did it. You got free of that nasty mother of yours. You'll have a long recuperation on the quiet beaches of Dover. In your case, it's all turned out quite well."

Sorcha allowed herself a small smile. "I am in your debt."

Julia stretched magnanimously. "And soon it will all be over," she reassured Sorcha. "Our trip is nearly at an end."

Sorcha turned her eyes to the window. A strong sense of foreboding twisted at her stomach. Whatever Julia was planning, she had a sense it was coming soon.

Chapter 12

The sun was drifting toward late afternoon, Julia kept poking her head out her window, and Sorcha wasn't surprised when Julia waved her hand out the window to Jonathan. He dutifully came up to ride alongside the carriage.

Julia's smile could melt lead. "Jonathan, my darling. I think I would like to stop and get out here. The views of the cliffs are just spectacular. You and I could take them in together. The rest of these three can ride down to the house and get settled in."

Cold fear coursed through Sorcha's veins. She immediately leaned forward. "I've never seen the cliffs! Surely I can come take a look."

Julia's gaze narrowed. "You'll have plenty of other opportunities to –"

"But not my first ever time! I want to be there. I want to see what there is to see."

Julia drew her eyes over Sorcha for a long moment, calculating. Then her gaze sharpened. "Yes, I do think you should come along, too. That would do nicely."

Jonathan shot a look of concern at Sorcha, but it was too late. The two women were climbing down out of the carriage.

Percy looked up sleepily. "Are we there?"

Julia smiled fondly at him. "You'll be home soon, dear. Don't forget to give Theodoria her medicine. I'll be along shortly."

He nodded, settling back in against the seat. "Of course, of course." In a moment he was snoring again.

Sorcha held her tongue as she closed the carriage door on the couple. New thoughts were whirling in her mind. No doubt Julia had arranged to have her sister drugged, as part of keeping her docile for this arranged marriage. It would all fit with Julia's pattern. Sorcha was only fortunate that Julia had not started in on drugging her. Sorcha knew she'd need all of her wits sharp for whatever Julia had planned.

Julia turned to the driver. "Carry on! We'll walk the rest of the way."

He nodded in understanding. With a flick of his reins the carriage was in motion again, rambling its way down the gently curving path.

Jonathan came down off his horse. He smiled at Julia, but Sorcha could see the tension in his shoulders as he walked between the two women across the meadow. "It's about five miles from here to your sister's house, yes?"

Julia nodded serenely. "Yes, not far at all. It'll be a nice walk once we take in the view, and I'm sure they'll have hot food waiting for us in the end." She turned to smile sweetly at Sorcha. "And you're so right, Sorcha my dear. You really should take in this sight of the cliffs. You never know what tomorrow might bring."

Sorcha gave a wry smile. *Or yesterday.*

They walked along the edge of the cliff for a while, taking in the ocean breezes, talking about the ball and what might be in store for the coming days. Jonathan trailed his horse behind him, maintaining a position between the two women. Sorcha was lulled into a sense of lassitude, into soaking in the beauty of a late autumn afternoon.

They rounded a corner.

The white cliffs of Dover were before them.

Sorcha drew in her breath. She had heard so much about them, and even so, they were stunning. The white chalkiness of their surface stood out stunningly in the sunshine, bright against the darkness of the water far below.

She stared at them in wonder. "Oh, they are truly beautiful, Julia!"

She smiled in contentment. "I know."

There was a movement from a stand of birch nearby, and Felton stepped out.

It took Sorcha a moment to absorb the scene. They were standing on the edge of a cliff-face, overlooking a steep drop, with not another soul in sight. Percy and Theodoria had long since departed in the coach. A scattering of woods lay before them, and Felton approached with a sharp smile on his lips. His hand floated at the knife at his hip.

His voice was low with amusement. "Imagine coming across you here."

Jonathan took a step in front of Sorcha, shielding her from Felton. His voice was low and terse. "Get on the horse."

Julia's hand darted out, as quick as a snake, grabbing Sorcha's wrist and hauling her near.

"Oh, I don't think so. Sorcha will be staying with me."

Felton nudged his head at the glistening cliffs. "Take one last look at that, my friend. Because your little run of a treasured life is about to come to a tragic end. It's my turn, now. I've been waiting a long time for this."

He wet his lips. "A lifetime."

In one quick motion he drew his knife and slashed. Jonathan jumped back, and the blade narrowly missed his midsection.

Felton laughed. "You're quick, I'll give you that. But I bet you've never been in a fight." He launched again, this time for Jonathan's chest, and Jonathan slipped it to the left.

"You're right," growled Jonathan, his eyes sharp with focus. "I've not been in a fight. But I've dreamt about them most every night."

Felton's brow creased with confusion. "Wha-"

Jonathan's right fist snapped out, thrown from his shoulder, and it connected solidly with Felton's temple. Felton staggered back in surprise, bringing a hand up. It came down smeared with blood.

Felton's brows drew together in billowing rage. All semblance of civility left his face.

"Right then, you bastard. Let's have it."

He plowed in like an enraged wild boar.

Julia's face glowed with vicious delight as Felton's blade connected with Jonathan's shoulder, gouging a ragged rip. She threw both fists in the air in a victory cry. "Get him, Felton! Stab him through the heart!"

Freed from Julia's grasp, Sorcha dove forward, striving to grab at Felton, but Julia spun and slammed her elbow hard into Sorcha's throat. Sorcha sprawled back onto the hard ground, searing pain sending all semblance of thought into a distant realm. She grasped at her throat, choking for breath.

There were heavy grunts, heart-rending groans, and solid thuds. Julia's screams of exhortation rang over it all, urging Felton on.

At last Sorcha's vision drew into focus and she rolled onto her side. She gasped at what she saw. Felton's face and arms were mottled with bruises and welts. His nose was twisted and bleeding. But Jonathan looked worse. Felton's knife had done its job, carving red gouges in Jonathan's chest, arms, and face.

Sorcha looked between their eyes. She could see it in each's man's gaze. Each would fight as long as he had breath left to draw.

Felton swung a whistling swipe at Jonathan, barely missing his chest, and Jonathan backed up a half-step. Felton repeated.

Sorcha furrowed her brow. Why was Felton not trying to make contact? It was almost as if …

She gasped, taking in the scene more fully.

Felton had worked Jonathan around to a promontory. While Felton and his partner-in-crime were on the main cliff face, Jonathan was now standing on a four foot square outcropping of stone. Felton had him cornered. If Jonathan lost his footing, he would plummet over the edge to his death.

Julia's eyes gleamed with avarice, her voice bright and harsh. "Do it, Felton. Do it! And the world will be ours!"

Felton's body shone with sweat, and his eyes were hard marbles. They stared into Jonathan's. "You'll scream like a banshee when you go down," he snarled. "You'll scream as you've never screamed before - because you'll know you've lost everything."

Sorcha's throat seared in agony, but she forced herself to stagger to her feet. She looked wildly around her, searching for something … anything …

Jonathan's horse.

The steed had shied down the path, given the violence going on. His reins trailed on the ground. Sorcha was torn between not wanting to spook him and reaching him in time to save Jonathan.

Time was almost gone.

She raced.

Some distant part of her brain screamed in staggering pain, but it was a far-off dream she knew she had to outrun.

Julia burst into peals of laughter. "And there she goes, Jonathan. Your lady love, fleeing, saving her own hide." She turned to Sorcha, her teeth bright. "Run, rabbit, run! We'll catch you soon enough." Her eyes turned predatory. "And then you'll join your boyfriend here. Together at last."

Sorcha put her foot into the stirrup and climbed up. She wheeled the steed to face Jonathan and the others.

Jonathan was weaving in place, blood streaming from a jagged cut over his right eye. The eye was nearly closed. Wounds and gouges riddled his body. His right arm was held close, protecting his ribs. She wondered how many were broken.

Jonathan nodded at Sorcha, his gaze steady. He opened his mouth to speak, but only a hacking cough emerged. It didn't matter - she knew exactly what he was trying to say.

He wanted her to flee. He wanted her to get to safety.

Felton laughed in triumph. "I've been waiting for this my entire life, you bastard. Dreaming about it every night. And now I'll finally feel it. The sensation of my knife driving deep into your heart."

He raised his blade high.

Sorcha kicked hard at the horse's side. The steed's powerful body surged into motion.

She drove straight at Felton and Julia.

The two raced down the coastline, fleeing …

There were high-pitched screams that seemed to go on forever …

The horse was rearing up, thrashing, trampling …

She clung to the mane with all her might …

Time hung still …

An eternity later, a strong hand grabbed the reins, settling the horse, calming him down. Then steady arms took a hold of Sorcha, gently lowering her to the ground. A strong chest drew her in, and she was held close as tears streamed from her eyes.

Jonathan's voice had a deep rasp, and he spoke between deep draws of breath. "It's all right, my love. Everything is all right."

Epilogue

Six months later

A warm May breeze drifted across the garden as Sorcha stepped out into the afternoon sunshine. She had been living with the Davenports for six long months, and had come to appreciate each season, but today was a special treat. The family was out shopping and it was just her and Jonathan for the afternoon.

She smiled as she came up to the table set with ivory linen and rose petals. He had truly outdone himself this time. A decanter of white wine sat to one side and an assortment of scones, puddings, and delicacies were laid out.

Her eyes lit up. "Is that haggis?"

Jonathan grinned. "Thought you might crave a little taste from home. Biddy has been practicing for weeks to get it right."

She laughed. "You really did go all out."

He poured out two glasses of wine and held his up in a toast. "To you, and to the joy you've brought to my life."

Sorcha smiled at him. "To both of us."

They clinked glasses, and she dug in.

The food was delicious. Butterflies danced amongst the roses, robins sang in the trees, and Sorcha wondered if she could ever be happier than this. It would have to take –

Jonathan stood, moved around to her side, and dropped to one knee.

Sorcha's mouth hung open. He couldn't be serious. She'd dreamt, of course. Every night. She'd treasured it as a hope. But was he actually –

He took her hand in his, looking up to her with depths that staggered her.

His voice was rough. "Sorcha, my darling, you've been patient with us these past six months. You've made an effort to settle in to our quiet life here. But I can see it in your eyes. You miss Scotland."

Sorcha's voice caught in her throat. She *had* missed it, desperately. She hadn't known it had showed. "I'm sure I can –"

He shook his head. And then he began to recite,

"My heart's in the Highlands, my heart is not here,
My heart's in the Highlands, a-chasing the deer;
Chasing the wild-deer, and following the roe,
My heart's in the Highlands, wherever I go.

Farewell to the Highlands, farewell to the North,
The birth-place of Valour, the country of Worth;
Wherever I wander, wherever I rove,
The hills of the Highlands for ever I love.

Farewell to the mountains, high-cover'd with snow,
Farewell to the straths and green vallies below;
Farewell to the forests and wild-hanging woods,
Farewell to the torrents and loud-pouring floods.

My heart's in the Highlands, my heart is not here,
My heart's in the Highlands, a-chasing the deer;
Chasing the wild-deer, and following the roe,
My heart's in the Highlands, wherever I go."

Sorcha soaked in the words. It was true. The vision of the quiet cottage on the highlands, of her and Jonathan side by side, still sung in her mind.

He twined his fingers into hers. "Sorcha, my love, you once told me you wished to see the world."

His gaze held hers. "I can offer you this. Marry me, and we shall have a cottage in the highlands. We shall go there for our honeymoon and soak in the heather all summer long. In the fall, we will gaze on the pyramids of Egypt. In the winter we shall explore the wineries of Tuscany. And in the spring, ah, in the spring …"

He brought her hand to his lips for a kiss. "In the spring we will return here, create our first-born child, and begin all over again."

Her eyes grew wide. "We could have a home here and in the highlands as well?"

He nodded, his eyes on hers. "I would do anything to make you happy. I would move mountains and whirl the stars into a cosmic dance."

She ran a hand down his cheek. "Then I shall be there at your side."

He seemed to hold his breath. "And that is a yes?"

"Yes, yes, yes!" And she laughed out loud as Jonathan stood and whirled her in a circle, lifting her off the ground. When her feet settled again, he looked down at her, his eyes deep and fathomless. His kiss reached into her very soul.

At last she drew apart. Her voice was a bare murmur. "This was perfect. Absolutely perfect. How did you know?"

He gave a wry smile. "I saw it in a dream."

Her mouth went round, and her eyes moved to the well. "Are they …?"

He nodded fondly, running a hand down her hair. "They are."

He glanced at the well, and he added, "It is May Day. And tonight is a full moon."

She took a hesitant step toward the well. It looked so simple – grey stone with a scattering of wildflowers along its edge.

Jonathan came at her side, his arm around her waist. He took a breath, then looked down into the depths.

His voice came out deep and resonant as he called down, "Hello!"

The echo rumbled, spun … and then there was a distinction – a response which sounded like him, and yet different. "Hello!"

Sorcha's breath caught. She twined her hand into Jonathan's and smiled.

Then she called out to her alter-self the question that had worried her all these long months.

"Happy?"

The echoes turned and tossed, and then there was a woman's response, warm, contented, full of rich delight.

"Happy."

Sorcha turned to Jonathan, drew him in, and the world fell away.

Thank you for reading *A Circle in Time*! The next stage of this series should start being live shortly.

If you enjoyed this novella, please leave feedback on Amazon, Goodreads, and any other systems you use. Together we can help make a difference!

Note that for those who prefer reading books in all-in-one form, each set of novellas will also be compiled as a completed box set once all are done. It just means you have to be patient and wait for me to finish writing all of them :). For those who prefer to read along as I write, and offer suggestions for me to shape the plot, these novellas are here for your enjoyment! Either way, I'd love to hear your feedback on the storyline and characters.

Be sure to sign up for my free newsletter! You'll get alerts of free books, discounts, and new releases. I run my own newsletter server – nobody else will ever see your email address. I promise!

http://www.lisashea.com/lisabase/subscribe.html

Please visit the following pages for news about free books, discounted releases, and new launches. Feel free to post questions there – I strive to answer within a day!

Facebook:
https://www.facebook.com/LisaSheaAuthor

Twitter:
https://twitter.com/LisaSheaAuthor

Google+:
https://plus.google.com/+LisaSheaAuthor/posts

Blog:
http://www.lisashea.com/lisabase/blog/

Share the news – we all want to enjoy interesting novels!

Dedication

To Ruth, whose enthusiasm keeps me going.

To the Boston Writer's Group, who supports me in all my projects.

To all my loyal fans who provide wonderful suggestions and advice for the continuing books in this series! I love integrating your ideas into my storylines.

About the Author

Lisa is an enthusiastic fan of regency-era England. She has sewn regency dresses and attended regency themed events. She has multiple copies of the Jane Austen, Emily Bronte, and other related books – as well as nearly all copies of those series available from movie or TV. The era seems to have just the right combination of elegance and passion.

She has a special place in her heart for England and Scotland. She has strolled along the coastline of Dover and walked along the Thames. She has gazed at the stones of Stonehenge and felt their power. She has soaked in the warmth of a Scottish tavern, enjoying haggis and whisky.

All proceeds from *A Circle in Time* benefit local battered women's shelters.

Lisa has written 39 fiction books, 81 non-fiction books, and 36 short stories.

Medieval romance novels:
Seeking the Truth
Knowing Yourself
A Sense of Duty
Creating Memories
Looking Back
Badge of Honor
Lady in Red
Finding Peace
Believing your Eyes
Trusting in Faith
Sworn Loyalty
In A Glance

Each medieval novel is a stand-alone story set in medieval England. The novels can be read in any order and have entirely separate casts of characters. In comparison, the below series are each linear and connected in nature.

Cozy murder mystery series:
Aspen Allegations | Birch Blackguards | Cedar Conundrums

Sci-fi adventure romance series:
Aquarian Awakenings | Betelgeuse Beguiling | Centauri Chaos | Draconis Discord

Dystopian journey series:
Into the Wasteland | He Who Was Living | Broken Images

Scottish regency time-travel series:
One Scottish Lass | A Time Apart | A Circle in Time

1800s Tennessee black / Native American series:
Across the River

Lisa's short stories:
Chartreuse | The Angst of Change | BAAC | Melting | Armsby

Black Cat short stories:
Lisa's 31-book cozy mini mystery series set in Salem Massachusetts
begins with:
The Lucky Cat – Black Cat Vol. 1

Here are a few of Lisa's self-help books:

Secrets to Falling Asleep
Get Better Sleep to Improve Health and Reduce Stress

Dream Symbol Encyclopedia
Interpretation and Meaning of Dream Symbols

Lucid Dreaming Guide
Foster Creativity in a Lucid Dream State

Learning to say NO – and YES! To your Dream
Protect your goals while gently helping others succeed

Reduce Stress Instantly
Practical relaxation tips you can use right now for instant stress relief

Time Management Course
Learn to End Procrastination, Increase Productivity, and Reduce Stress

Simple Ways to Make the World Better for Everyone
Every day we wake up is a day to take a fresh path, to help a friend,
and to improve our lives.

Author's proceeds from all these books benefit battered women's
shelters.

"Be the change you wish to see in the world."

As a special treat, as a warm thank-you for buying this book and supporting the cause of battered women, here's a sneak peak at the first chapter of *Into the Wasteland – A Dystopian Journey*.

Into the Wasteland - Chapter 1

"I will show you fear in a handful of dust."

-- T. S. Eliot, The Waste Land

I blink my eyes. The hallway is narrow, clinically clean, and crowded with an undulating line of men and women extending ahead and behind. We are uniformly garbed in tangerine-orange cotton outfits with short sleeves and long legs reaching down to sturdy leather boots. The cloth's color reminds me of Buddhist monks, peaceful, seeking alms along a quiet dirt roadway. But here the bodies are burly and scarred. Muscular arms are tattooed with swastikas and rough symbols I do not recognize.

The heavy-set man before me turns and glares; I take a step back. His small eyes skewer me for a moment longer before he settles into place again, shuffling forward beneath the glare of the fluorescent lights.

A reedy voice behind me pipes into my awareness.

"Hey there, young lady. Careful, now, he's a repeat."

I turn in confusion, my eyes sweeping down until I find him. He's perhaps five foot, rail-thin, his large eyes deep-set in a wasted skull. He nods to make his point, his gaze darting forward to the hulking form before us. "He's been here before," he insists.

"Been where?"

The hunched figure shudders, then glances ahead with trepidation. "Nodo."

The word means nothing to me, and I stare at him blankly.

An awareness brightens his eyes, and he looks me over with pity. "Chute blindness got to you? I've heard it happens. Well, your memory might come back eventually. Or it might not." The corner of his mouth quirks up. "Or the locals will blast a hole through you before you get a chance to find out."

There's a harsh voice to my left. "Strap on your belt. Your hand touches the grip before the doors open, and you die."

I look up in surprise. There's a sheet of safety glass to my left, a momentary disruption in the long wall of alabaster, and behind it sits an officer in full riot gear. A metal drawer pushes open toward me, and within it is a leather belt with a holster holding a snub-nosed .38 automatic. The magazine is in place.

I draw it out of the drawer, giving it a heft.

Fully loaded.

I strap it on my hip, my fingers settling the buckle with practiced ease.

I take a step forward, and behind me the thin voice bubbles in nervousness. "I've never used one of these before," he argues. "I don't know how –"

I turn, and the drawer is sliding shut, the gun and belt still within. I reach for it, snagging it out, holding it toward him.

My voice is tight. "What do we need these for?"

His eyes dart forward again. "For the wasteland," he mutters. "But I have never shot one of those. It won't do me no good."

I look down at the holster. It's a reversible unit. I flop it to the other side, then strap it on my left hip, overlapping the other. "Stay behind me," I instruct him.

He scurries closer to me, glancing around in nervousness. After a moment his voice comes, low, quiet.

"I'm Ragnor."

My mouth tweaks into a wry smile. "That makes one of us that knows who he is."

He gives a short bark. "It'll come to you," he promises. "In the meantime, we just have to survive these next twenty minutes. Tales tell that a full quarter don't make it past this first part."

I glance ahead to the bright white of the hallway, its length occupied by steadily moving bodies. "Oh?" The pistol station had been the only break in its length.

He nods. "The chute is the worst, from what I hear. The locals see our release as a Christmas of sorts – free offerings of fresh weapons, unused ammo, and a few pairs of boots and holsters. The cops have cleared the forest for perhaps two hundred yards, but that turns it into a no man's land. If we can make it across that, we'll be OK."

I glance back. "Then what?"

His eyes brighten. "Well, then we're loose in seventy thousand square miles of forest and frozen winter. All we have to do it is make it through the two-hundred-fifty miles north to the goal, and we're free. We get complete amnesty."

My brow raises. "Amnesty for what?"

He gives a wide smile. "I'm completely innocent of my charges," he promises. "I am sure you are too. This is all some sort of mistake."

A voice sounds from above, clinical, flat, and steady.

"Any convict who touches their weapon before the gates open will be shot."

Ragnor's eyes slide nervously to the guns at my hips. "They're serious," he warns. "Don't want to give them an excuse."

The room opens up before us into a chamber the size of half a football field. Orange-garbed people fill in around us, crowding forward, pressing us against the matte corrugated metal which lines the whole front wall. As the trickle slows, each person creates a space around them, perhaps two feet, settling, staring at that wall, easing their hand toward the weapon at their side.

Ragnor huddles behind me, peering at the metal with trepidation.

"They used to send prisoners out as soon as they were convicted," he murmurs, his voice tight. "But the locals picked them off too easily. It became a death sentence. Now the cops send us out in large groups. Figure the locals only cull out the weak and slow that way."

I feel the weight of the weapons on my hips, steady, sure. I stretch both hands wide, settling back my shoulders. I draw in a long, deep breath, absorbing the fear, sweat, and adrenaline coursing from all sides. I let out the air, my eyes focused with pinpoint precision on the metal ridges before me.

The gate rolls up.

Bright sunshine glints off the hulk of a burnt-out black limousine etched in rust. I dive for its cover, Ragnor tight behind me. Shots zing out overhead, and the heavy-set man at my left screams in agony, clutching his shoulder. I peer through the shattered windshield. The scene before me is chaos incarnate. Piles of tires smolder in low flames, sending billows of charcoal smoke high into a pale blue sky. The ground is dirt and gravel, spattered with blood, bits of leather, and the occasional bone. All around me people are screaming, shots are ringing out, and a burst of crimson shows where a bullet met its target.

I glance back. A three-story-high wall of smooth concrete stretches to either side, as far as the eye can see, marking a border of my new world. The back wall in the chamber we had come from pushes forward, evicting the few stragglers who scream in frantic panic. Another few sharp retorts and their corpses spin and fall, splaying on the soft dirt.

The metal gate slides closed.

Ragnor scuttles back to one of the bodies, digs at his side, and then comes forward to join me again.

I look ahead to where a large rectangle of plywood lays angled over a mound of dirt. I nudge my head at it, and he nods. I send two shots forward, and then go racing for the cover. There's the tang of a bullet just past my ear, but we make it there safely.

I drop to my stomach and poke my head around the edge. A burly man wearing a coon-skin cap is fifty feet ahead, his pock-marked face red with exertion. He is carefully aiming a pistol to his left, drawing a bead on a gangly convict with pale eyes.

I steady my pistol with my left hand, draw in a breath, then hold it for a moment. I focus on his chest and squeeze.

Pop.

I raise the pistol to his forehead, his eyes now wide with surprise, and pull again.

Pop.

The body falls, limp. In a moment I'm in motion, racing forward to the clump of twisted metal beams he had been crouching in. It might have once been a shed.

Ragnor's voice is tight behind me. "Why'd'ya shoot him twice?"

My eyes scan the terrain ahead. "Once in the chest - a large target to take him down," I explain. "Then once in the head, in case he's wearing a vest."

The forest line is only a short distance ahead, birch and oak nestled in fall foliage colors. The crimson and orange make a complimentary counterpoint to our outfits and the bursts of blood which are exploding all around me.

A shot tangs past us on the left, and I spin, shooting twice, taking out a dark-skinned woman with a jagged scar across her forehead. Then we sprint hard, our lungs bursting with the effort, and make the tree line.

Safe.

I take nothing for granted. We stay in motion, pushing hard, delving further into the shadows. We climb over rotting logs and slog through tumbling streams. The sounds of battle drift far behind us, the quiet rustle of the forest fills our ears, and at last the blood eases its thundering in my chest. We have been in motion for at least a full hour.

We have escaped the welcome net.

Ragnor's tense face widens into a smile as we step into a quiet clearing. "Seventy-five percent!"

I smile at that. "It seems so," I agree.

There is a rippling stream before us, nestled amongst the white birch, and my throat is parched.

I step forward to the bank, looking down in its clear water. There is a shallow by where I stand, and the smooth surface gives me my first real glimpse of myself.

My hair is long, perhaps to my mid-back, and dark brown in color. Gentle waves give it some texture. My skin is tan, although from the sun or nature I cannot tell. My eyes are wide-set, deep brown, and steady with focus. My body within its orange uniform is slim, with round breasts and slim hips. I appear to be in my early twenties.

I give a soft shrug, and the figure before me shrugs back. It will have to do.

I drop easily to a knee to drink in the fresh water.

A single shot rings out high overhead, a distinctive zing with an echoing reverb. I throw myself flat on the sandy bank.

There is a groan behind me, and I turn my head. Ragnor is splayed back against the moss, his blond hair askew, his left hand clutching at the dark crimson stain which is spreading steadily across the tangerine orange of his shirt.

Here's where to learn what happened next!

http://www.amazon.com/Into-Wasteland-Dystopian-Journey-Ishtato-ebook/dp/B00MX242E8/

Thank you so much for all of your support and encouragement for this important cause.

Be the change.

52883888R00068

Made in the USA
Middletown, DE
26 November 2017